FINDING HER FEET

EVE AINSWORTH

Illustrated by
LUNA VALENTINE

Barrington Stoke

To my niece Lily – a kind and creative superstar with the biggest heart. Keep being amazing.

First published in 2023 in Great Britain by
Barrington Stoke Ltd
18 Walker Street, Edinburgh, EH3 7LP

www.barringtonstoke.co.uk

Text © 2023 Eve Ainsworth
Illustrations © 2023 Luna Valentine

The moral right of Eve Ainsworth and Luna Valentine to
be identified as the author and illustrator of this work has
been asserted in accordance with the Copyright, Designs and
Patents Act, 1988

A CIP catalogue record for this book is available
from the British Library upon request

ISBN: 978-1-80090-202-2

Printed in Great Britain by Charlesworth Press

CONTENTS

CHAPTER 1

THE TROUBLE WITH SCHOOL

Lily wasn't sure how she was meant to feel about school. The other people around her seemed to find school easy, but for Lily it always felt like she was an outsider. She never really fitted in.

It was even harder now that Lily was in Year Seven and at secondary school. It was huge compared to her small primary, and she felt very overwhelmed.

There were girls from her old school, like Beth Mayhew and Olivia Gate, who had found new friends easily. But Lily had always struggled with making friends. She never knew how to talk to people she didn't know or make herself seem interesting.

Beth used to be Lily's best friend, but that had been back in primary school. Here it was different. Beth was now hanging out with Amelia Ross, who was loud and confident. This meant Beth was now one of the popular ones. Her friendship with Lily had been forgotten fast.

Beth and Amelia were always huddled together, talking and laughing with some of the other popular girls. Sometimes they looked over at Lily and she wasn't sure if they were laughing at her or not. So now Lily was often alone. She sometimes wandered the playground trying not to look bothered or found an empty spot in the library where she would read by herself.

Lily didn't want to tell anyone how she felt. Not even her dad. She knew he would be

concerned and would probably phone the school, and Lily didn't want to give him more to worry about. Lily's dad had been working flat out to look after them both ever since her mum had left over five years ago.

Her dad still thought she and Beth were best friends and had no idea that Lily spent so much time alone. He'd noticed a few things were different, especially since Beth no longer came over to their house, but Lily had told him that Beth was busy with clubs and things. She found it was easier to change the subject than to face more questions from him.

Lily was good at pretending everything was OK. No one could see the nervous twisting in her stomach. The sick, hot flushes that she got in school were something she could keep to herself.

Lily also thought she was good at blending into the background. She probably would have kept doing so if Mr Allen, her PE teacher, hadn't asked to see her after class at the end of the day.

It seemed that someone had noticed Lily after all.

"Is everything OK, Lily?" he asked.

Lily scowled. She wasn't really sure what to say. How would Mr Allen understand what she was feeling?

"I've noticed that you've been on your own a bit," he went on, smiling gently. "And you seem sad."

Mr Allen was one of those teachers who never seemed to get angry or stressed. Most of the time Lily really liked him, especially as PE was one of her favourite subjects. Mr Allen often gave her lots of praise. But right now she felt awkward. Did she really want to admit that she was feeling lonely? How would that make her sound?

And would Mr Allen really understand about the worrying thoughts that buzzed in her head like a mass of bees?

"I'm OK," Lily said, forcing a smile.

"You know you can talk to me if you need to?" Mr Allen replied softly. "I'd like to think I can help."

"How?" Lily couldn't stop herself asking.

Mr Allen grinned and said, "Well! Let's just see, shall we? I've recently set up a girls' football team."

He passed her a leaflet. It had the title "Lightmoor Lionesses" and a photo of two girls running down a football pitch. "We train twice a week after school and play games on Saturdays. Some of the other girls in your year have joined up. Beth and Amelia for example. I think you will really enjoy it."

"But I can't even really play football," Lily said, feeling confused.

"You'll learn fast, I'm sure," Mr Allen said. "I can tell you have potential. I've seen you in PE. You're fast and have great co-ordination."

"But …" *I might make a fool of myself*, Lily was thinking. But she didn't say that. She could see that Mr Allen was keen for her to give it a go.

"It's a great way to gain confidence, to make new friends," he said.

"Really?" Lily said.

She thought about how her stomach always twisted in knots when she worried about coming to school. About her lonely walks down the school corridors, wondering if the other girls were talking about her. She was so tired of feeling like an outsider. She wanted something to change.

"I suppose I could give it a try," Lily said finally. Her finger traced the picture of the girl on the leaflet. She looked so happy. "I'll have to ask my dad if he can take me."

Lily had a feeling her dad would be pleased about this. He was a massive football fan, and they had often kicked a ball about together in the garden and at the park. Her dad had tried to talk Lily into joining a football team before, telling her that she had a natural talent for the game. Lily had never been sure if she should believe him. After all, her dad was lovely to her about everything ...

"What have you got to lose?" Mr Allen said. "You never know, you might enjoy it."

Lily remembered Mr Allen saying that Beth played for the Lionesses. Maybe this way she would start hanging around with Lily again.

She glanced at the leaflet in her hands. For the first time in ages, a bit of hope fluttered inside of her.

Maybe she could do this? Maybe she could be part of a girls' football team?

THE ROOTS OF WOMEN'S FOOTBALL

Over 100 years ago, a young woman called Nettie Honeyball helped to kick-start women's football in the UK. She placed an advert in newspapers saying she was looking for players for a women's football team. Nettie persuaded around 30 women to sign up.

This was the start of the British Ladies' Football Club. The training sessions were held twice a week in a park in Hornsey, North London.

Nettie was a young feminist and believed that women should be able to play the same sports as men. She said that she started the women's football club because she wanted to prove to the world that women "are not the ornamental and useless creatures that men have pictured".

In 1895, the first British Ladies' match took place at Nightingale Lane in Crouch End in London. It was watched by over 10,000 spectators (a great number for that time in history). It was a match featuring players from London and the surrounding areas – which meant it became North London versus South London.

The game was criticised by many. The *British Medical Journal* even published an article claiming that football could expose women to "violence" and damage their organs!

The British Ladies' team went on to play lots of games but continued to get lots of criticism. Sadly, money problems meant that the club was closed down a few years later.

Women's football did not really come into the spotlight again until the start of the First World War and the introduction of another amazing group of women.

More on that soon ...

CHAPTER 2

GOOD ENOUGH?

Lily's dad pulled up in the car park at Lightmoor's ground. This was the same place where the men and boys played. It was pretty impressive, with a decent training pitch to one side and a small ground and spectator stands on the other.

Lily's dad had been talking all the way, telling Lily about the times when he used to play football as a young boy.

"I loved it. There's nothing like being in a team," her dad told her. "It makes you feel part of something important."

"But what if I'm not good enough?" Lily asked.

Other questions were whizzing around her head too. Questions that Lily didn't want to worry her dad with – such as, what if the other girls didn't like her? What if they were mean and left her out?

What if this was all just a really bad idea?

"You've played a lot with me in the back garden, haven't you?" said Lily's dad. "I've seen what a decent left foot you have."

"Yeah, but that was just messing around ..." Lily replied.

Her dad ruffled her hair. "You'll be fine. Relax and enjoy it – that's the most important thing. You might even surprise yourself."

"Do you think?" Lily asked.

Dad grinned at her. "I know so." Then he lowered his voice, and his eyes had that look that meant he was being serious. "You need to believe in yourself, Lily Moore," her dad said. "You can do anything if you put your mind to it."

Lily walked slowly over to the group of girls around Mr Allen and another man she didn't know. They were doing stretches that she recognised from PE lessons. Lily knew that her cheeks were already glowing red. She could feel her tummy flip flop as all their eyes looked up to meet hers.

Mr Allen threw his arms up as soon as he spotted her.

"Lily, you came! Brilliant!" he said, and gestured towards the group. "You'll get to meet everyone during the session, but I think you already know Beth and Amelia from school."

Beth had been tilting her body into a side stretch, and she flashed Lily a weak smile. It

wasn't exactly the friendliest of greetings.
Amelia was standing next to Beth, but she didn't
even look towards Lily. Lily noticed that Amelia
was dressed in a kit that looked expensive.

"I'm going to pair you up to do some passing
exercises," Mr Allen continued. "Lily, you can go
with Beth as you know each other already."

Beth walked over to Lily slowly. She looked a bit annoyed and distracted. Lily felt something tug inside her. She remembered how the two of them used to go to each other's houses after school and have sleepovers at weekends. They would sit in Lily's bedroom and share secrets and silly jokes. They'd been so close, and now Beth could hardly look Lily in the eye.

"I'm glad I've been paired with you," Lily said.

Beth smiled a little. "I was surprised to see you here," she said. "I didn't think you liked this sort of thing?"

"Well, I like football ..." Lily said hesitantly. Beth knew this already. They had played together plenty of times in the park, pretending they were going to be the next England stars. "I guess I'm just a bit nervous. I've never played properly, and I don't know if I'll be any good."

Beth shrugged and replied, "Just try your best. That's all I try to do."

"Well, sometimes you're not too bad, Beth. When you manage to keep up."

Amelia had drifted over. Her sharp tone seemed to be directed at Beth, which surprised Lily – wasn't Beth meant to be part of Amelia's popular group now?

"I'm not the fastest, that's true ..." Beth muttered.

"Don't worry, it takes time to become a proper player," Amelia said, her voice now overly sweet. Her gaze moved to Lily. "Some people might never get there, sadly."

"Amelia!" Mr Allen warned. "Remember we are a team here. I don't want any nasty comments. Please make Lily feel welcome."

Lily felt like the ground was about to open up under her, but then she remembered her dad's words. She just had to believe in herself, that was all.

She just had to try her best.

The first training exercise wasn't too bad. Lily could control the ball and move it back to Beth fairly easily. However, Beth was now acting like being paired with Lily was the worst thing in the world.

Beth pulled a face every time she kicked the ball. Her attention kept going back to the other girls – in particular, Amelia, who was laughing loudly and being pretty silly most of the time. Lily couldn't help but wonder why Amelia had called herself a "proper player". A lot of the time she seemed to find it hard to kick the ball properly. It looked like it was all just a bit of a laugh to Amelia.

After the warm-up, Mr Allen gathered the group together and told them they would play a match. He split them into two teams. Lily was with Beth again. Amelia was on the opposing side.

The girls picked their positions fast. But Lily felt unsure, not wanting to put herself forward for a certain position. A smaller girl with red hair and freckles placed a hand on her shoulder.

"I noticed you play with your left foot a lot," she said. "Would you like to play wide on the left wing?"

Lily nodded. "That would be good."

The girl smiled. "I'm Emma," she said. "I'll be on the right wing. Hopefully we can link up."

The game started, and Lily was unsure what to do at first. The only football she had ever played was in the back garden with her dad or mucking around in the park with Beth, but she had watched plenty of matches on TV.

Mr Allen also coached Lily from the sidelines. He reminded her that as a winger she had to keep wide and use speed to get round the defenders.

Lily didn't see much of the ball at the beginning. The girls weren't used to passing to her. However, about five minutes in, Lily found herself in lots of space. Emma had the ball.

Lily suddenly felt a surge of confidence.

"Emma! Here!" she called.

Lily wasn't used to shouting, and she felt heat rush to her cheeks. But Emma didn't seem to notice. She looked up and whipped the ball over to Lily.

Luckily, Lily had time and space to control the ball. She could see Beth was just outside the penalty area. Lily ran, not giving herself much time to think. She kept the ball close to her feet like her dad had taught her.

Beth shouted for Lily to pass.

Lily whipped the ball in her direction, hoping she had timed it right.

Beth managed to control the pass with her chest and then volleyed the ball cleanly in the direction of the goal.

A shout went up.

They had scored. 1–0. And Lily had assisted.

She felt a rush of excitement as the other girls ran to congratulate her. Even Beth managed to grin in her direction.

Amelia picked up the ball, scowling. "That was lucky," she hissed at Lily. "You only managed to do that because you were in so much space."

"It was a great pass, Amelia," Beth told her.

Amelia shrugged and said, "If you say so, Beth. At least it's nice to see you score for once. Maybe you've finally learned how to play."

Lily noticed how pale Beth's face had gone, but Beth said nothing and instead walked away, her shoulders dropping.

Lily couldn't help but feel shocked. Weren't Beth and Amelia close friends?

Why was Amelia being so mean?

THE DICK, KERR LADIES

During the First World War, women had to take on demanding jobs to help with the war effort as so many men were away fighting. They worked on the railways and in factories, as well as working on the land, helping to grow food.

In the north-east of England, many women worked in munitions factories, which supplied troops with weapons and equipment. The most famous was the Dick, Kerr & Co. factory.

This was hard and dangerous work. The heavy machinery caused lots of injuries, and women were exposed to dangerous chemicals in the explosives. The chemicals turned their skin yellow, and the workers were nicknamed "the Canaries".

The women were encouraged to play sport in their break-times to help build their strength and wind down from the struggles of the day.

It was during these break-times that the Dick, Kerr factory women began to play football together. A lot of them had played in the streets with their brothers, so they were already pretty skilful.

As a joke, some of the women challenged the young boy apprentices who were still working in the factory to take part in skills challenges. One challenge was to kick a ball through a small window in the cloakroom. Many of the women were better at this than the boys – including Alice Kell and Grace Sibbert.

A clerk named Alfred Frankland saw how talented they were. He encouraged the women to set up a football team of their own and the Dick, Kerr Ladies F.C. was born. The idea was that they would play local charity matches and raise money for injured soldiers.

The organisers hoped that there would be a bit of interest in the team. Nobody could have imagined just how important and popular they would become ...

CHAPTER 3

PART OF THE GROUP

As the weeks flew by, Lily discovered she was really enjoying training. The sessions were great fun and she was able to pick up the skills fairly quickly.

Mr Allen was pleased with Lily's performance and told her that she would be able to play in a proper tournament soon.

"You've made really good progress," he said, patting her on the back. "I can see how well you fit into the team."

And Lily did seem to fit in! Apart from Amelia, the other girls were keen to chat and helped Lily feel part of their group.

At home in her back garden, Lily showed Dad the tricks she had learned. These included how to turn with the ball, how to do a step-over and how to fake a move to send the defender on the wrong foot. Her dad was impressed.

"You're turning into a proper Lily Parr," he said.

Lily didn't have a clue who Lily Parr was, but she looked her up on her phone and was impressed. Lily Parr was one of the greatest footballers of her generation, and she was listed in the National Football Museum's Hall of Fame. They shared a name. Was it fate? Perhaps Lily could be just like Lily Parr.

For the first time in ages, Lily couldn't feel that flutter of worry in her stomach. Instead, she felt a flutter of something else.

Excitement!

Even at school, things were better. Beth was now talking to Lily and always smiled when she saw her. Lily wished that she could sit with Beth at lunch-time as well, but maybe that was a step too far. She didn't want to seem pushy.

"You're a really good addition to the team," Beth told Lily after a training session. "I'm glad you joined us."

Lily was glad too. She had also been added to the team's social-messaging group. She liked reading the excited messages between the girls. It felt nice to be included in something at last, even if she was still the new girl.

She still felt a bit lonely sometimes at school, but at least now she had the excitement of her next training session to look forward to. Lily sometimes looked over at Beth at lunch, sitting with Amelia and the other girls. Was it her imagination or was Beth always on the edge, looking slightly out of place?

Lily was beginning to wonder if Beth was as happy in her new friendship group as she had thought.

*

At the next session, Mr Allen made the girls dribble the ball between cones, then take a shot at goal.

Lily found it easier to control the ball with her left foot. Sometimes the ball ran away from her, but she stayed patient and learned to roll it back into position, moving carefully so that the ball stayed with her.

She wasn't the fastest player, but she did OK and enjoyed blasting the ball into the back of net. She also loved watching Beth and Emma, who both ran as if the ball was glued to their feet.

"Don't worry, keep practising and you'll soon be the same," Emma told Lily kindly.

Lily really liked Emma. She wished they went to the same school. Emma was so kind and friendly but was also an amazing footballer.

"I want to be as good as you," Lily told her.

Emma smiled. "I'm sure you will be. The secret is practice, and to never give up."

After the session, Mr Allen gathered all the girls together and praised them for their hard work and commitment.

"I'm so impressed, I've decided you are ready to play your first match in two weeks," he said. "It will be against another girls' team, the Panthers. They have been around for a long time, and they know their stuff, so they'll really put you to the test."

There was a ripple of excitement as this news was processed. Emma was beaming from ear to ear.

"The Panthers are amazing," she whispered to Lily. "It's really hard to get into their team. I can't believe we're getting a chance to play against them."

"Won't they destroy us?" one of the other girls asked nervously.

"Not necessarily," Mr Allen said. "We'll have a practice match next Saturday to prepare, but I can already see that you are playing like a team. The passing and movement off the ball has been wonderful to watch. I really think you have a chance of winning this game. There have been some standout performances."

He stepped forward and tapped Emma lightly on the shoulder. "Emma has worked tirelessly on the wing today and hardly mistimed a cross," Mr Allen said. "Beth has been superb up front, fighting for every ball. Frankie has battled and fought in defence, and our new girl – Lily – has shown speed and intelligent passing."

Lily felt her cheeks burn as the girls' eyes turned to her. She wasn't used to this much attention. Most of the team were murmuring praise. Emma even squeezed Lily's arm as if to say, "I told you so". There was only one girl who did not seem as happy.

Amelia.

"Yeah, well, some of us never get the ball passed to us ..." she muttered.

Lily knew this wasn't fair. The other girls often passed to Amelia, but she had a habit of holding on to the ball for too long or losing it.

"Mr Allen thinks you're good too," Beth said softly, clearly trying to reassure Amelia. Beth laid her hand on Amelia's arm.

Amelia shrugged it off. "Easy for you to say," she snapped.

Lily saw the hurt flash in Beth's eyes, and some of the happiness Lily had felt began to melt away.

New fears were gnawing inside her. How would she perform in a proper game? What if she messed up? What would happen then?

EARLY SUCCESSES FOR WOMEN'S TEAMS

Several new women's football teams were formed during the First World War, but the Dick, Kerr Ladies continued to be one of the most well known. Soon the team became very successful, against all expectations.

The fast and skilful play of the Dick, Kerr Ladies meant their games drew in huge crowds at grounds such as Goodison Park, Old Trafford and Stamford Bridge. They also raised significant amounts of money for charity – what would be millions of pounds in today's money.

The Dick, Kerr Ladies were also the first women's team to travel abroad, when they were invited to play a French side in 1920. They were also the first team EVER to play at night – with a white ball and floodlights supplied by the War Office.

On Boxing Day 1920, the Dick, Kerr Ladies played their biggest game ever at Goodison Park, home of Everton FC. More than 53,000 spectators packed into the ground. Another 12,000 people were unable to get inside and had to stand in the surrounding streets. This was the largest crowd ever for a women's non-international game and was proof of their growing popularity.

The Dick, Kerr Ladies team included amazing players such as Alice Kell, Jessie Walmsley and Grace Sibbert. But the standout player was Lily Parr. She is still thought of as one of the greatest footballers of all time. She was just 14 when she joined the team and had a great left foot. She scored 986 goals in her 30 years playing for the club and was the first female player to be included in the National Football Museum Hall of Fame.

The Dick, Kerr Ladies are now considered one of the best football teams of all time, with an impressive winning streak.

At the height of their success, it seemed like women's football was on the rise and the only way was up. But sadly, not everyone felt the same way ...

CHAPTER 4

DRAMA ON THE PITCH

"What if I mess up, Dad?" Lily said. "Then I might not get picked to play against the Panthers."

"You won't," her dad replied. "I promise. Just enjoy the practice session, Lil. Go out there and try your best. That's all anyone can ask of you."

They had just arrived at the ground. Lily's dad seemed more excited than she was about the upcoming match. He had been helping her work on her ball control and shooting skills all week.

"Remember today is just for practice," Lily's dad reminded her. "Mr Allen will want to try out a few things and see how you girls do. It's nothing to worry about."

Lily grabbed her water bottle and managed a weak smile. "I guess not," she replied.

Lily's dad reached over and ruffled her hair. "Seriously, Lil. This is the happiest I've seen you for ages. Keep enjoying yourself, OK? That's all you need to do."

Lily left the car feeling a lot lighter. Her dad was right. Since starting to play football, she hadn't had that horrible twisty feeling in her stomach so much. And she hadn't been feeling so panicky.

She ran towards the other girls, feeling uplifted when she saw their smiles.

This was supposed to be fun. She had to remember that.

As always, the training session began with some warm-up exercises. Lily was paired with a girl called Brooke, who had always been nice and welcoming. She was also an excellent defender. They worked together on passing the ball quickly between their feet, and Brooke told Lily that she hadn't been in the team for long herself.

"Did you play somewhere else before that?" Lily asked.

"Only with my older brothers," Brooke replied. "But I was much better than them. That's why my mum decided to find a club for me."

"I've never really played before either," Lily confessed. "I watch games all the time with my dad, but I never thought I was good enough to play."

Brooke drove a shot hard at Lily, and she controlled it with her left foot and passed it back.

"Well, you're wrong about that, aren't you?" Brooke said, grinning. "If you ask me, you're a natural."

Mr Allen arranged the practice match between the girls to get them prepared for the following weekend. He divided them into two sides. Lily was put in the same team as Amelia,

Brooke and Beth. For the first half, Lily was on the wing again. Amelia was on the bench. Lily heard Amelia complain about this, but she tried to ignore her. Lily didn't want anything to put her off.

"We all have to sit out sometimes," Brooke said to Lily quietly, out of earshot of Amelia. "Besides, Amelia was rubbish this morning. She wasn't concentrating."

Lily did feel a bit sorry for Amelia, but she knew that Brooke was right – Amelia had spent most of the morning talking loudly and messing around. Mr Allen must have seen that.

The game was a fast one and the girls were clearly keen to impress their coach. The ball was driven up the middle of the pitch towards Beth a lot of the time. She was looking sharp and determined. It wasn't long before Beth picked up a sweet pass from Brooke, turned neatly and drove a shot into the bottom corner of the goal.

Within minutes of that goal, Lily received the ball out wide. It was the first time she'd had a clear run with the ball. Lily had space, so she moved fast, taking care to keep the ball close to her feet. Looking up, she saw that Beth was being closely marked, and there was no one else free.

Lily hesitated for a moment, not sure what to do. But then she heard her dad's voice in her ear.

"Just go out there and enjoy it."

Lily struck the ball. She didn't dare look as her heart lifted along with the shot.

Had she made a mistake?

The ball curled and looked as if it might be dipping into the top corner ... But then, at the last moment, the ball clipped the bar and spun over.

Lily froze, frightened that her teammates might be cross at her for missing, but instead they rushed over to her, their faces bright with smiles.

"Amazing shot, Lil!" Brooke shouted.

"Unlucky!" Lola added.

"That was really good, Lil," Beth said. She ran over to Lily and patted her on the back.

Lily felt her tension melt away – until she looked towards the sidelines and saw Amelia looking sulky.

It was clear that one person on the team wasn't so happy with her performance.

We're on the same side, Lily thought as she ran back to the wing. *So why doesn't it feel like that?*

For the second half of the game, Lily was on the bench. She was fine with that – after all she was still the newest member of the team. Mr Allen told her that she had done really well in the first half.

It was fun to watch the other girls as they played together. From the sidelines, Lily could see just how talented some of the players were. How strong Emma was in defence. How fast Brooke was. How quick-footed Beth was.

Amelia had replaced Lily on the wing. She wasn't very fast, but she was fearless and not afraid to go into a tackle. Beth had been switched to the other side and was now playing against Amelia.

The game was still 1–0 as Mr Allen's phone rang. He told the girls to keep playing and moved away from the pitch a little.

Lily could see that Amelia was getting frustrated with Beth, especially as Beth was able to slip the ball away from Amelia easily. It wasn't long before Beth scored another goal to bring the two sides even.

There were only minutes to go, and Lily was beginning to feel relieved to be near the

end. She could see Amelia was getting angry –
shouting at the other girls and kicking the ball
away when she made a mistake. It felt like
something dramatic would happen at any time.

And then it did.

With only moments left, Amelia had the
ball and was making a last-ditch attempt to
run down the wing. There was just one player
up against her – Beth. Lily was the only person
who had a clear view of the action.

Beth moved fast, sweeping across the pitch.
She made a hurried but clean slide tackle that
took the ball away from Amelia.

Amelia fell to the ground.

And then all hell broke loose.

Mr Allen came off his phone and rushed to
Amelia. She was now on the ground, clutching
her leg and screaming in agony.

"Beth did that on purpose," Amelia screamed. "She took me out. She's hurt my ankle."

Beth stood to one side. She looked upset, and she was chewing on her lip. The rest of

the team were rushing towards Amelia, full of sympathy and concern. One of the taller players, Deena, gave Beth a sour look.

"That was dirty," she hissed.

Lily felt frustration rise inside her. She rushed over to the group. They hadn't seen the tackle as clearly as she had. They didn't understand!

"It was a clean tackle," Lily said loudly. "Beth took the ball. She didn't mean to hurt Amelia."

"Don't, Lily ..." Beth said, her face hard.

"But you didn't mean it! I could see. You did the right thing. You—"

"Just stop trying to get involved, will you?" Beth said loudly, her voice shaking. "Just leave me alone."

And she marched off the pitch.

BANNED!

By 1920, women's football in England had become very popular, but not everyone was happy about it. Lots of petitions and campaigns were started to try to bring an end to women playing the game.

Critics claimed that football was not ladylike and was damaging to women's health. There were also concerns that women's football was becoming more popular than men's – and some people felt that could not be allowed to happen.

So, in 1921, the FA made the brutal decision to ban all women's football, meaning that they could no longer play on pitches that were approved by the FA. The reason the FA gave was that "the game of football is quite unsuitable for females and should not be encouraged".

The Dick, Kerr Ladies were now forced to play on non-FA pitches or abroad (where they were still welcomed). This limited crowd size and restricted what female players could do.

The ban on women's football stayed in place for over 50 years, meaning that it was held back for half a century!

Can you imagine the outrage it would have caused if that had happened to men's football?

CHAPTER 5

ALL CRASHING DOWN

Beth wasn't at school the next day or the day after. Lily was worried that she was still feeling bad about what happened at the game.

On top of that, the team chat was full of messages. Lily had opened the first one – posted by Amelia:

Beth was out of order – taking me out like that. It will take me weeks to recover. I don't know what her problem is?

And the new girl can back off too. Why is she sticking up for a dirty player? Do we really want her on the team?

The first reply was from Deena who "totally agreed" with Amelia's message

Lily didn't dare read the rest of the messages, but she could imagine they were all just as angry and nasty. She muted the group chat, but it was too late to fight the anxiety that was beginning to build inside her.

Had she done the wrong thing speaking up?

And where was Beth? Why wasn't she in school?

*

Back at home that evening, Lily felt like she couldn't face the rest of the team at training.

What might they say to her? Would they even want her there?

"I can't go to training, Dad," Lily said. "I have a really bad tummy ache."

Dad frowned. "Really? That seems a shame."

Lily pulled the cushion closer to her stomach as if to make the point clearer. Beside her, the phone brightened with a notification. Unread messages were still waiting to be opened, but Lily couldn't bring herself to look at them. She was still thinking about Beth and why she hadn't been at school. Beth had been so angry at Lily for trying to defend her and now it seemed like the rest of the team were too.

Lily just felt so exhausted by it all. For the first time in ages it had felt like she belonged somewhere. She had enjoyed what she was doing. Now it seemed as if it was all crashing down around her.

"Lily, are you sure you're OK?" Dad asked gently.

Lily couldn't stop it. The tears were fighting to escape, and she was soon blurting out the whole story to Dad.

"I've ruined everything," Lily sobbed. "I can't go back to football now."

Dad pulled her into his arms. "You haven't ruined anything," he said firmly. "You stuck up for your teammate. That's what being part of a team is all about."

He squeezed her tighter. "I'll talk to Mr Allen, and we'll get this sorted. Don't you worry. But you need to go to training tonight. You can't run away from these kinds of things."

But that was easy for her dad to say. All Lily could do was worry.

And all she could see whenever she closed her eyes was Beth's angry face.

*

Mr Allen was waiting with Amelia and Deena when Lily arrived at training. Lily could feel her anxiety begin to build, but Dad nudged her forward. There was still no sign of Beth.

"Lily," Mr Allen said, smiling. "I'm glad you made it."

Lily nodded, not sure what else to say.

"I heard there were some words said after the game at the weekend," he continued. His eyes drifted towards Amelia, who was looking down at the ground. "I wouldn't want that to put you off," Mr Allen added.

"I was a bit rude," Deena said. "I was upset because Amelia got hurt. From where I was standing, Beth's tackle looked messy." She turned to Lily. "I shouldn't have sent that message on the group chat. That was wrong."

"It's OK," Lily said.

She was glad Deena had apologised, and she did seem like she meant it.

Amelia looked up. Lily could see she looked really upset. Amelia shifted towards her, and Lily noticed she was still struggling with her ankle.

"I was out of order too," Amelia said quietly.

Lily looked around her. There was still a gnawing feeling in her stomach that wouldn't go away.

"Where's Beth?" Lily asked.

Mr Allen frowned. "I'm not sure, Lily. It's not like her to miss training. I just hope she's at the match on Saturday. I'm sure she wouldn't want to miss that."

It was a good training session. They worked on fitness and stamina. Lily enjoyed the sprints more than anything. She came third against Emma and Ruby, but she felt like her strength was building all the time.

Amelia couldn't join in because of her ankle, but she stood on the sidelines cheering the girls on. Instead of scowling, Amelia was smiling a bit.

"I'm sorry about your injury," Emma said to Amelia as they were packing up to leave. "I hope you're not out for too long."

Amelia looked a bit sheepish. "Well, I did exaggerate it a bit on the group chat to try to make Beth feel bad. It's only a strain, and it was hurting before she even tackled me. I was pushing myself too hard to try to impress Mr Allen."

"Well ... I'm glad you're going to be OK," Emma replied. "But I'm not sure why you were trying to make Beth feel bad."

Lily didn't understand either – it was no way to treat a friend.

Amelia just shrugged. "She can be annoying sometimes, that's all," she said, before walking away.

Emma turned to Lily. "It was nice of you to stick up for Beth like that," she said. "All of the girls were impressed, you know! They were more annoyed at Deena and Amelia for making drama."

"They were impressed with me?" Lily said, confused. "I thought I'd upset everyone."

Emma shook her head. "Have you not read the messages?" She dug out her phone and passed it to Lily.

Lily scrolled through the posts and could hardly believe what she was reading.

Lily – well done for speaking up!

Lily, you've done nothing wrong. It was a fair challenge.

Lily – you're a star. Welcome to the team.

Lily's head was spinning.

"But what about Beth?" she asked quietly. "She was so angry at me for speaking up."

Emma shrugged. "I think Beth has a lot of stuff going on right now. Amelia probably hasn't helped, always trying to outshine her." Emma paused. "Give her time. I think she could use a friend like you right now."

MOVING ON – HOME AND AWAY

In 1965, the Dick, Kerr Ladies team disbanded,
but many other female teams played on.
They continued to strive to succeed despite
the FA ban.

In 1969, the Women's FA was formed (WFA), and
the first Women's FA cup final and first England
Women's international were held within three
years. By 1994, the Football Association had taken
over the WFA national league and set up its own
Premier League.

In 1997, the FA announced that it would develop
women's football from grassroots to elite level, and
in 2001, they were promoting football as a sport
that women should consider both at school and
later on in life.

The drive to develop women's football certainly
seemed to be working as in 2006 England qualified
for the World Cup and went on to reach the
quarter-finals.

Women's football was growing internationally too, and in America it had been building for some time.

In the 1999 Women's World Cup final, 90,000 fans crowded into the stadium to watch the hosts USA beat Chile on penalties. Then in 2013 the National Women's Soccer League kicked off in the USA. Over the years it would showcase some of the best female talent in the world, including superstars such as Australian striker Sam Kerr and American legend Alex Morgan.

Other countries were also creating successful international women's teams, such as Germany, France, Spain, the Netherlands, South Korea, Australia and Norway. The popularity of the female game was building worldwide.

Was women's football finally back on track?

CHAPTER 6

THE BIG MATCH

It was the day of Lily's first match. She was buzzing with excitement. Her dad gave her a big hug at the ground.

"Remember I'm here cheering you on," he said. "And I'm proud of you whatever happens."

Lily smiled up at her dad. There had been times when it had been hard, being just the two of them. But today she knew her dad was all she needed.

*

The girls huddled together for a team talk before the game. Lily was disappointed to see that Beth still wasn't there. Had she left the team?

"I heard Beth's really poorly," Brooke said. "But no one knows for sure."

Without Beth upfront and Amelia in midfield, their team was weaker. It also meant that Lily had to play.

"Don't worry," Emma said to her. "You can do this!"

Lily tried to ignore the familiar flutters of nerves and worry in her stomach. She looked around at her teammates. She soaked in their encouraging smiles. They were like rays of sunlight beaming at her.

She'd got this.

The whistle blew.

Lily felt like the butterflies in her stomach had been replaced by fire. She found herself calling for the ball as she sprinted against an opposing player. She made a few tackles, and within a few minutes Lily had driven a good ball across the face of the Panthers' goal. Sadly, the Lionesses' striker couldn't quite reach the ball to steer it into the net.

The Panthers were hard and fast and had most of the possession. It wasn't long until their number 11 picked up the ball on the left and made a wide, sweeping run, soon placing the ball neatly at their striker's feet. She took a touch, looked up and hit a fierce and deadly shot into the far corner of the net. The Lionesses' goalie, Sienna, had no chance.

The half-time whistle blew. 0–1.

Some half-time drinks and a team talk renewed the Lionesses' enthusiasm.

Lily's heart was racing as they returned to the pitch. She could hear Mr Allen encouraging their team on. She could also hear Amelia shouting from the sidelines. Lily glanced over at the small crowd and could make out her dad standing there watching her.

"I'm so proud of you ..."

Lily fought on. She picked up every loose ball and tried hard to win back every ball they lost to the Panthers. Yes, she was one of the least experienced members of the team, but it didn't stop her trying – despite getting bruised and battered.

Determination drove Lily on.

Finally, she managed to take the ball from the Panthers' number 12. Lily looked up and saw Brooke was in space. Quickly, she lifted the ball over to Brooke, who spun and volleyed the ball neatly past the diving keeper.

1–1.

The whistle blew for full time.

Lily felt like her lungs were about to explode. Her head was pounding, and her legs were like jelly. She rushed to join the other girls for a group hug and realised she had never felt happier – or more alive – in her life.

Football really was the best thing she had ever done.

*

On Monday, Lily walked into school feeling different, lighter somehow. Or was it just more hopeful? On the way in, she had been reading the messages from her teammates. They were still so excited about the game and talking about the next fixture. Lily felt fully included now. She felt she belonged.

And even better, Lily realised she wasn't that bad at football. She could make a difference. She could be part of something special.

"Hey, Lily!"

She looked up surprised and saw Beth jogging towards her. Lily's heart lifted. Beth was smiling. She clearly wasn't angry at her any more.

"I heard about the game yesterday," Beth said. "It sounds like you played a blinder. I'm sorry I missed it."

"Where were you?" Lily asked.

Beth frowned. "Oh, it's been a horrible week," she replied. "My mum was really ill. She was taken into hospital, and ..."

She flapped her hand and added, "It's OK. She's getting better now, but I was so worried. That's why I wasn't at school or training."

"I'm so sorry," Lily said. She shook her head, feeling silly now. "I thought it was me. I thought it was because you were angry with me ..."

"What – about the tackle?" Beth laughed. "No! I was angry at myself. Amelia had been winding me up all day, and the truth is I went into the tackle wanting to bring her down. I lost my head. That wasn't good. I was only cross with you because you were being too nice to me. I didn't deserve it."

"Well, Amelia was being hard work that day," Lily said.

Beth shrugged. "She's all mouth. I don't know ... I used to think Amelia was funny and good to hang around with, but now I'm not so sure."

"Really?"

"Yeah," Beth said, her smile widening. "I reckon I have better friends, don't you?"

Lily grinned back. "I dunno – maybe?"

Beth pulled Lily towards her, linking arms with her. "Come on," Beth said. "Let's go inside. You'll have to sit with me at lunch. I want to hear all about the match. We can talk about the next one against Marshbrook too – I've heard they're really tough in defence."

The two girls walked in together, with all talk focused on football. Lily was more than happy with that.

Lily had finally found her feet.

THE LIONESSES

At the beginning of the 21st century, things had really started to look up for women's football. We now have a new generation of young players that are at the top of their game.

Players like Mary Earps, Georgia Stanway, Lauren Hemp and Alessia Russo are now making names for themselves both at club and international level.

In 2022, the England Lionesses won the European Championship in spectacular fashion, introducing a new group of exciting players to the game, along with many new fans.

Before this, the England team had qualified for the European Championships eight times, reaching the finals twice.

England had also qualified for the World Cup six times, reached the quarter-final three times and the semi-finals twice. They finished third in 2015.

It's an amazing time to be a female football fan or player. However, female football players are still fighting for equal pay and recognition. We need to continue to shout their names loud, support them and be part of the movement to get women's football back on an equal footing to men's – where it belongs.

The future is certainly brighter, whether you are a player, a fan, or just someone who believes in equality, but we must never forget the struggles of the past, and we must continue to fight to keep women's football where it belongs. At the top!

Our books are tested
for children and young people by
children and young people.

Thanks to everyone who consulted on
a manuscript for their time and effort in
helping us to make our books better
for our readers.